Growing Together

words by **Ruth Spiro**
pictures by **Paola Escobar**

HARPER
An Imprint of HarperCollinsPublishers

HarperCollins Children's Books, a division of HarperCollins Publishers,
195 Broadway, New York, NY 10007

HarperCollins Publishers, Macken House, 39/40 Mayor Street Upper,
Dublin 1, D01 C9W8, Ireland

Growing Together
Text copyright © 2026 by Ruth Spiro
Illustrations copyright © 2026 by Paola Escobar
All rights reserved. Manufactured in Capriate San Gervasio, Italy.
No part of this book may be used or reproduced in any manner whatsoever without written permission except in the case of brief quotations embodied in critical articles and reviews. Without limiting the exclusive rights of any author, contributor, or the publisher of this publication, any unauthorized use of this publication to train generative artificial intelligence (AI) technologies is expressly prohibited. HarperCollins also exercises their rights under Article 4(3) of the Digital Single Market Directive 2019/790 and expressly reserves this publication from the text and data mining exception.
harpercollins.com

Library of Congress Control Number: 2025937061
ISBN 978-0-06-323776-6

To create the digital illustrations in this book,
the artist captured her love for plants in Adobe Photoshop.
25 26 27 28 29 RTLO 10 9 8 7 6 5 4 3 2 1
First Edition

For my family, with all my love.
Hang on, little tomatoes!
—R.S.

For my beloved friend Lorena.
We have planted and grown together.
—P.E.

It's springtime! It's green time!
You need room to grow.
Your new home is waiting.
Ready? Let's go!

Here we are—it's our garden!

There's something new.
The Swiss chard and spinach . . .

and a spot just for you!

All those who help out share the fruits of our labors.

Come dig in the dirt with your friends and neighbors!

First, till the soil.

Next, pull the weeds.

Then mix in the compost,

and plant seedlings and seeds.

Sprinkle some water,
and now that we're done . . .

a sweet, juicy treat—
berries warm from the sun!

Peas in their pods
on a long, leggy vine
hold on to a fence
or trellis or twine.

To pick the top pods,
we need the whole crew.

These plants are climbers,
just like YOU!

Boiled or pickled
or baked till they're sweet,
the bountiful, beautiful
beet can't be beat!

Just like us, these flowers are hard at work too.

They bring bees and butterflies . . .

and what do *they* do? They search in the flowers for something to eat. Inside, they find nectar, their favorite treat.

Pollinators are friends.
We want them to stay.

Let's welcome them into our flower buffet!

From spring rolls to sweet tea,
I do love my . . .

mint!

How does a vegetable play hide-and-seek? It waits underground until you take a peek.

Green feathered leaves with a root that goes *crunch*,

we'll pick it

and wash it

and eat it for lunch!

Hold on, tomato, it's almost your time. Until then, stay close to your friends on the vine.

A gardener is patient.
A gardener can wait.
Hold on, tomato,
you're doing just great!

A zillion zucchini are ready today! We'll keep what we need and then give some away.

Our summer's-end harvest gives plenty to share.
A meal among friends.

Please, pull up a chair.

Some dishes are familiar,
others are new.
Their one thing in common?
All use plants that we grew.

See our sunflowers soar?
The sky's not the limit!

Our garden's a happier place with you in it!

TOGETHER WE GREW:

Greens/Swiss Chard
There are many types of healthy greens to try. Some Swiss chard plants have rainbow-colored stems!

Strawberries
Strawberry plants grow on long vines called runners.

Peas
Pea plants have tendrils that curl around anything they can find to support the plant as it grows.

Beets
The ball-shaped beet is the root of the plant. It stores nutrients from the soil that help the plant grow. Both the root and the greens are edible.

Pollinators
When bees, butterflies, and birds enter a flower to drink its nectar, powdery pollen from the flower sticks to their feet and bodies. As they move from flower to flower, the pollen helps the plants form fruit and seeds.

Herbs
Herb plants come in many different shapes and sizes. Their leaves are used for cooking, as tea, and even as medicine.

Carrots
Carrots grow underground because they are the root of the plant. The tops can be eaten too.

Tomatoes
The tomato has seeds and grows from the flower of the plant. This means it's not a vegetable but a fruit.

Zucchini
In late summer, these plants grow many yellow flowers. The flowers with a large bump at the bottom are the ones that grow a zucchini behind them.

Sunflowers
Sunflowers can grow to eight feet tall or higher! Birds love to eat the seeds, and the bright yellow petals attract bees.